Storybook Treasury of
Animals

STORYBOOK TREASURY OF ANIMALS published in 2003 by Grosset & Dunlap.

BABY WHALE: Text copyright © 1991 by Lynn Wilson. Illustrations © 1991 by Jean Cassels. BABY CHIMP:
Text copyright © 1996 by Debra Mostow Zakarin. Illustrations copyright © 1996 by Betina Ogden. HORSES:
Text copyright © 1997, 1987 by Margo Lundell. Photographs © 1987 by Harold Roth. BABY ELEPHANT:
Text copyright © 1997 by Lucille Recht Penner. Illustrations copyright © 1997 by Betina Ogden. ALL ABOUT
DOGS AND PUPPIES: Text copyright © 1998 by Grosset & Dunlap. Photographs © 1998 by Elizabeth Hathon.
ALL ABOUT CATS AND KITTENS: Text copyright © 1999 by Emily Neye. Photographs © 1999 by Elizabeth Hathon.

Library of Congress Cataloging-in-Publication Data is available.

ISBN 0-448-43332-X   A B C D F G H I J

Storybook Treasury of

Animals

By Laura Driscoll, Margo Lundell, Emily Neye, Lucille Recht Penner,
Lynn Wilson, and Debra Mostow Zakarin

Illustrated and photographed by Jean Cassels, Elizabeth Hathon,
Betina Ogden, and Harold Roth

GROSSET & DUNLAP

Table of Contents

ALL ABOUT
Cats and Kittens

By Emily Neye
Photographs by Elizabeth Hathon

Did you know that cats are the most popular pets in the world?

It's easy to see why. Cats are smart, loyal, and affectionate. They also can be very entertaining!

Cats have lived with people for thousands of years—that's as long ago as the time of the ancient Egyptians! At first, people kept cats because they were so good at catching pesky rats and mice. But soon, people started liking cats for other reasons—the same reasons people love cats today. They make us smile. They keep us company. They are our friends.

Unlike dogs, most adult cats are about the same size and shape. But they can still look very different from one another. Some cats have short fur. Some have very fluffy fur. There are even some cats that don't have any fur at all!

Different types of cats, or *breeds*, have different kinds of coats. There are *shorthaired* breeds, like the Bengal. And there are *longhaired* breeds, like the Persian.

SPHYNX (HAIRLESS)

BENGAL

PERSIANS

Cats' coats come in many colors, too. They can be solid or patterned. A *tabby* cat has a striped or spotted coat. A *pointed* cat has ears, paws, tail, or face that are in different colors from the rest of its body.

Cats are experts at climbing and leaping. Their flexible bodies can twist and turn at amazing angles. And their long tails help them keep their balance.

This cat uses his strong hind legs to push off. Look how high he can leap! It's easy for him to reach his favorite hiding place.

Cats have no trouble walking along narrow fences and ledges. They are as graceful as the best tightrope walkers.

When cats do fall, they almost always land on their feet. While they are in the air, they twist their bodies and whip around their tails until their feet point downward. Cats don't think about doing this while they are falling. They are just following their instincts.

Cats are mammals, just like people. This means that after a mother cat gives birth to kittens, she feeds them milk from her body.

There are usually four or five kittens in a *litter*, or family. The newborns are tiny and helpless. When they are born, their eyes and ears are sealed shut. But their little noses are working! The kittens will depend on their sense of smell to find their mother's milk.

After about a week, their eyes and ears begin to open. And within three weeks, the kittens will begin to walk around and play. But they still need their mother for food and protection. This kitten has strayed too far away! Her mother lifts her up by the scruff of her neck to carry her back to her brothers and sisters.

Kittens from the same litter can be different colors. They can have different personalities, too. Some kittens are shy and some are frisky.

Did you know that every kitten is born with a different nose-print? Just like our fingerprints, no two nose-prints are alike!

Kittens need to stay with their mother for at least eight weeks after they are born. During that time, they grow and learn a lot. By watching their mother, they learn how to groom themselves. And by "play fighting" with each other, they learn how to hunt.

They also learn on their own—just like these curious kittens!

Young kittens shouldn't be adopted by human families right away. But they should have contact with people from the time they are about four weeks old. The more used to people they become, the better pets they will make.

Having a pet cat is a big responsibility. The kitten you bring home could be a part of your family for as long as twenty years! During that time, it will need lots of attention and love.

A young kitten should be fed four small meals every day. Older cats will probably only need one or two. Remember, cats need food made just for cats. Dog food and table food won't have all the nutrients your cat needs to stay healthy. Cool, fresh water should be available at all times, too.

Most cats love cream, like these two kittens! But it should be given only as a special treat—too much can upset a cat's stomach.

If your cat is going to be kept indoors, you will need to train it to use a litter box. Cats are smart, so they usually catch on quickly. But be prepared for accidents!

You should keep the litter box in a quiet place, away from where your cat eats. Be sure to clean the box every day.

Cats clean themselves by licking their fur all over. Their rough tongues are covered with tiny spines—the spines work just like the teeth on a comb!

To clean its face, a cat licks its paw and then rubs it over its head.

But cats don't always groom themselves as well as they should. So they still need a regular brushing to get rid of loose hair and tangles. Longhaired cats, like Persians, need to be brushed at least once a day.

Just like you, your cat needs to visit the doctor for a checkup about once a year. Animal doctors are called *veterinarians*.

When you adopt a cat or kitten, you should take it to the veterinarian first thing—even before you take it home. The vet will make sure your cat is healthy and give it shots to protect it from diseases.

During checkups, the vet will examine your cat all over. He will look in your cat's ears. And he will listen to your cat's heartbeat.

A healthy cat should have a moist nose, clear eyes, clean ears, and a glossy coat. If you notice a change in the way your cat looks, you should take it to the veterinarian as soon as you can.

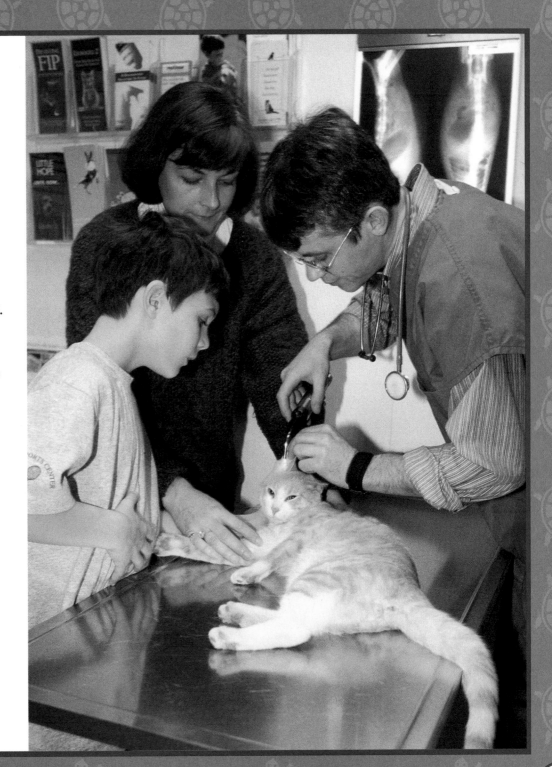

Cats need to exercise in order to stay fit, just like we do. Most cats don't like to be walked on leashes, but some don't mind!

As long as you have safe toys around, and make time to play together every day, your cat should stay trim.

A scratching post like this one works like a jungle gym, too. Not only will it keep cats busy, it also might save your furniture. All cats will scratch objects to stretch their legs and to keep their claws clean. So it's a good idea to train your cat to use a post, rather than the sofa!

Even though cats cannot speak, they can tell you how they are feeling in other ways.

A happy cat will purr and partially close its eyes.

An angry or scared cat will arch its back and puff up its fur, so it looks bigger. It may hiss or scream, too.

When a cat rubs up against you, it is saying, "We are family."

Cats have special glands around the face and near the base of the tail that produce odors. Even though cats may not smell strongly to us, they can tell one another apart with one sniff. By rubbing up against you, your cat marks you with its special scent. Now she, and other cats, will recognize you as part of her family.

Cats mark their territory in the same way. When your cat rubs up against the furniture in your house, she is leaving behind a message to other animals. The message is: "This space belongs to me!"

You may notice that your cat spends a lot of its time dozing. Cats sleep up to sixteen hours a day! But they do not sleep for long stretches at one time. They just take short naps throughout the day and night. That's where the term "catnap" comes from.

Some people enter
their cats in cat shows.
A cat that is shown in
a cat show must be
purebred, which means
its mother and father
are of the same breed.
There are forty-five
official breeds in cat
shows today.

The owners spend a lot
of time preparing their
cats. They are very proud.

Judges give a cat points for its coat, body, health, and personality.

This cat is a real champion—look at all the ribbons she has won!

But we don't need ribbons to tell us that our cats are special. They show us every day. Whether your cat is independent, playful, or shy, she is bound to be. . .

. . . full of surprises . . .

. . . and full of love.

ALL ABOUT
Dogs and Puppies

By Laura Driscoll • Photographs by Elizabeth Hathon

Can you imagine a world without dogs? It's not easy. These days dogs are just about everywhere you look! They're in homes across the country and around the world. They star in movies and TV shows. They work in real life as guard dogs and police dogs. They're even in our history books! Did you know that the first living creature to visit outer space was a dog?

Dogs and humans have been good friends for at least fourteen thousand years. That's a long time. So it's no wonder dogs make such good pets. They've had lots of practice.

Dogs come in all shapes and sizes. There are very big dogs and very small dogs. There are dogs with floppy ears and shaggy fur, dogs with pointy ears and short fur, and dogs of many different colors. It all depends on what type, or *breed*, a dog is.

Each dog breed belongs to one of seven groups.

Working dogs include breeds that work as police dogs, guard dogs, search-and-rescue dogs, and sled dogs. These important jobs call for brave, smart dogs that can recognize and obey lots of commands.

Siberian Husky

Great Dane

Rottweiler

Border Collies

Herding dogs can be trained to herd sheep or cattle, and to protect them from wild animals.

Shetland Sheepdog

Welsh Corgi

Greyhound

Hounds are good trackers. Some hounds use their extra-strong sense of smell to follow animals over very long distances, or to help the police find missing people.

Irish Wolfhound

Norwegian Elkhound

Airedale Terrier

Terriers have long been used by hunters to chase animals out of underground holes. Many terriers have a patch of long fur on their chin that looks like a little beard.

West Highland Terrier

Norfolk Terrier

Sporting dogs are used for bird hunting. Some, like setters and pointers, sniff the air and then point with their bodies to show hunters where birds are hiding nearby.

Hungarian Vizsla

English Setters

English Cocker Spaniel

Nonsporting dogs are kept mainly as pets today, even though some of them were used for hunting or herding many years ago.

Bulldog

Bichon Frise

Dalmatian

Toy dogs are the smallest breeds of all.

Yorkshire Terrier

Chihuahua

Cavalier King Charles Spaniel

All of these dogs are called *purebred* dogs. Purebred dogs are dogs whose mother and father are of the same breed. But many dogs are *mixed-breed* dogs—they are a mix of two or more breeds. A mixed-breed dog might look like its mother in some ways and its father in others.

Dogs are mammals, like we are. After a mother dog gives birth to puppies, she feeds them with milk from her body and watches to make sure each puppy gets enough.

A family of puppies born together is called a *litter*. Puppies are born with their eyes and ears sealed shut. At first, they can only feel and smell their way around. Then, about two weeks after they are born, the puppies' eyes and ears open up.

Puppies in the same litter might be different colors.
And they might be different in other ways, too.

In this litter, one
puppy is very
independent.

One puppy stays
close to its mother.

The other puppies
are very playful.

If you want to get a dog or puppy of your own, there are a few things to think about first. Like any pet, a dog is a big responsibility. It will need to be fed and walked every day, and taken to the doctor when it is sick. Will you be able to give a dog a happy, healthy, and loving home?

There are so many different kinds of dogs to choose from. Some breeds need lots of exercise. Some breeds bark more than others. Some breeds are small all their lives, while others will grow up to be almost as big as you are! So think hard about what kind of dog you want.

Where can you get a dog of your own? One place to look is the animal shelter, where there are always healthy dogs waiting for a good home. Or if you want a puppy, maybe you know someone whose dog just had puppies.

You will probably want a puppy that is between six and eight weeks old. Puppies this age are old enough to leave their mother and go to live with their own human family. Look for a playful and active puppy with clear, bright eyes and a clean, shiny coat.

Young puppies need to be fed three or four times a day in small amounts. There is special puppy food made just for them. Puppies also need lots of cool, fresh drinking water, kept out all the time in a bowl they cannot tip over.

If a puppy misbehaves, its owner must say "No!" in a stern voice. She never ever hits her dog. And when it does obey her, she rewards it with big hugs and lots of praise.

Dogs of all ages should be brushed often. But dogs should have a bath only when they really need one, because too many can dry out their skin. Some dogs love baths. Others hate them. Either way, wet dogs like to shake themselves dry—so watch out!

Time for a walk! Most dogs need at least two walks a day to stay healthy. Walks are good exercise, and dogs usually like them because it's a chance for them to see other dogs.

Just like people, dogs need to visit the doctor for a checkup about once a year. An animal doctor is called a *veterinarian*. In the waiting room at the vet's office, dog owners sit with their dogs, petting them and talking to them softly to keep them calm. Sometimes it's hard for a dog to stay calm with so many other dogs around!

Inside the exam room, the vet checks everything—from the dog's eyes and ears to its toenails and feet. The doctor also might take the dog's temperature and listen to its heartbeat.

What a healthy dog!

Dogs haven't always looked the way they do today. In fact, thousands of years ago, they looked more like wolves. Wolves and dogs are very closely related to each other. In the wild, wolves live together in groups called *packs*. In every wolf pack, there are two wolves—one male and one female—that are the leaders of the pack, and all the other wolves follow and obey them.

In some ways, dogs are still a lot like wolves. If a dog sits when its owners says "Sit!", it is because it thinks of its owner as the leader of the pack. Some dogs are happiest when they are following instructions from their owners or trainers—whether it's playing fetch with a ball, working as a search-and-rescue dog, or herding sheep.

Herding dogs are some of the hardest working and most helpful dogs around. Sheep farmers use whistles, hand signals, or voice commands to tell the dogs where they want the sheep to go. Then the dogs go to work.

The dogs in these photographs are Border collies. One Border collie can herd up to one thousand sheep on its own!

Everybody knows that Dalmatians are fire dogs. But do you know why? In the days of horse-drawn fire engines, fire departments adopted Dalmatians because of their bravery and their ability to get along with horses. Sometimes, on the way to a fire, the dogs would run along next to the horses, barking and clearing the way for the fire engine. Those days are long gone, but even today many fire departments keep Dalmatians as pets.

At dog shows, beautiful dogs compete for awards. The judges look at a dog's coloring, body shape, and size. They choose one dog of each breed to get the "Best of Breed" award. The judges also pick a "Best in Show" dog—the one that they like best of all the dogs at the show.

At this neighborhood dog show, every dog is a winner! The judges have award ribbons for the Cutest Dog, the Friendliest Dog, the Most Bashful Dog, the Most Unusual Dog, and lots more! There are enough awards so that each dog gets one, because as every dog owner knows, each dog is special in its own way.

Just like people, no two dogs are exactly alike. But most people love dogs for the same reasons.

They comfort us when we are sad.

They protect us.

They play with us.

They are family. . . .

They are our friends.

HORSES

An Abridgment of *Harold Roth's Big Book of Horses*

Text by Margo Lundell
Photographs by Harold Roth
Abridgment by Laura Driscoll

Long ago in America, horses were everywhere you looked—pulling coaches and carriages filled with people, hauling loads from farm to market, and delivering important mail.

Today, we have cars, trucks, and planes that take people and things from one place to another. Even so, we still see horses in many different places—at the fair, the circus, in the park, and running in horse races.

Most horses grow up on farms. A baby horse is called
a *foal*. In just minutes, a newborn foal can stand up and take
some wobbly steps over to its mother. The baby will stay
very close to its mother until it is about six months old.

A one-year-old horse is called a *yearling*. Yearlings are about half as big as adult horses—and twice as frisky!

A two-year-old horse is like a teenager. It is as tall as it will get, but its muscles and its bones are still developing. A horse is an adult when it is five years old.

There are certain things that make horses very happy. Most horses love to run just for the fun of it. In wide-open pastures, they gallop from one end to the other, glad to be out in the open. Sometimes mother horses, like the one in this picture, challenge their foals to a race by running on ahead of them.

Horses like to roll around on the ground. This is just the thing for scratching an itch. It also covers the horse with a thin layer of dirt, which protects against biting insects.

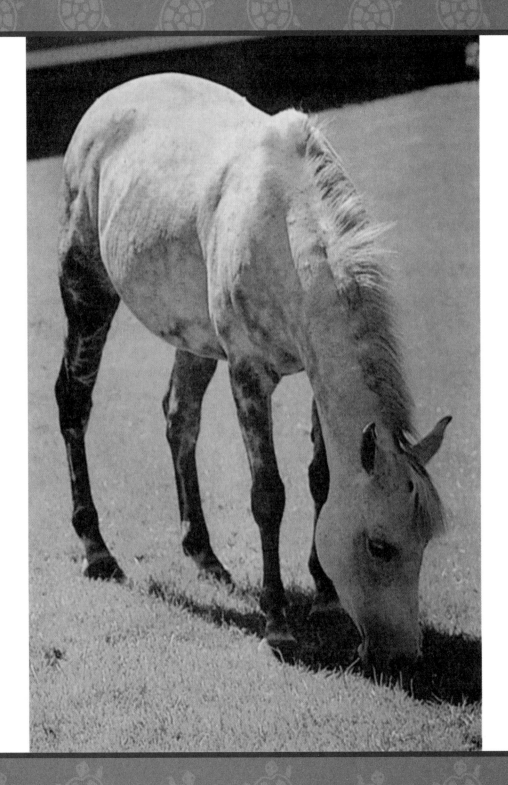

Horses also love to eat—especially oats, hay, grass, carrots, and sugar cubes for a sweet treat. They are called *grazing animals* because they like to eat often, but only a little bit at a time.

Horses comes in all shapes, sizes, and colors. It all depends on what *breed* a horse is. A breed is like a family of horses all related to one another.

Morgan horses are strong and fast.

Thoroughbreds are the fastest long-distance runners of all the breeds. Most racehorses are Thoroughbreds.

Arabian horses are famous for their beauty and speed. This is one of the oldest breeds we know of.

Most cowboys had *American quarter horses*. They were the most popular workhorses of the American frontier.

Appaloosas come in lots of different colors, but most of them have spots. So sometimes they are called "raindrop horses."

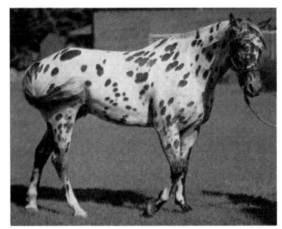

There are many kinds of *ponies*. Some people think ponies are small because they are baby horses. But they are not. All ponies, even adult ones, are small because that is just how their breed is.

Have you ever wondered what it would be like to have your own horse? Here is what an average day might be like.

Bonnie has a horse named Bambi. Early in the morning, Bonnie goes to Bambi's stable. She gives him a hello pat on the nose and some grass to munch on. Then Bonnie cleans the stall. She takes away any dirty straw or sawdust on the floor and puts clean sawdust in its place. The sawdust is a little easier on Bambi's legs than the hard floor.

Then it's time for breakfast. Bonnie brings fresh water, hay, and oats for Bambi.

Later on, Bonnie gets Bambi ready for a ride! First she *grooms*, or brushes, Bambi.

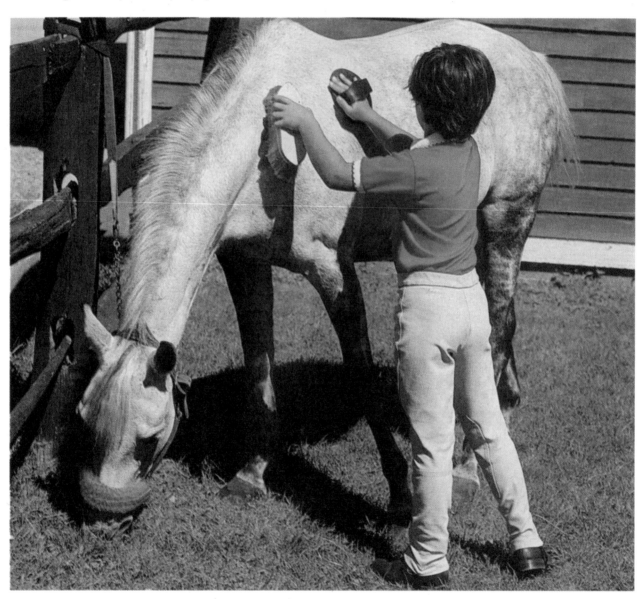

Bonnie also must scrape out any dirt or stones stuck in Bambi's hooves. Otherwise, he could get an infection or sore spots.

Finally, Bonnie and Bambi are ready to saddle up and go. They race down the long meadow together. There are many different ways riders can tell their horses what to do. Sometimes they pull lightly on the horses's reins. Sometimes they press on the horse's sides with their legs. Sometimes they use their voice. Every horse is different, and some like certain signs better than others.

On warm days, Bonnie gives Bambi a little shower after the ride. Then, she lets him graze in the meadow, while she cleans the saddle and the other riding equipment.

At the end of the day, Bonnie brings Bambi back into the stable and gives him dinner—more hay and oats and fresh water. Then Bonnie says good night and leaves Bambi to drift off to sleep in his stall.

Sometimes kids who have their own horses enter them in horse shows. Young riders have to show judges how their horses walk and run at different speeds. In some youth competitions, horses also show off their jumping skills. Jumping takes a lot of practice, but it's one of the most exciting events at a horse show.

In adult competitions, horses and riders jump over high fences, race on cross-country courses, and sometimes perform *dressage*, a series of very exact, small steps. The best horse-and-rider teams might get to go to the Olympics!

And they're off! At horse races, the faster horses speed around the track at about forty miles per hour! Racing fans flock to racetracks to see the colorfully dressed riders, or *jockeys*, and to cheer for their favorite horses.

This kind of horse racing has taken place for thousands of years. Sometimes it is called the "sport of kings" because many English kings and queens over the centuries have owned horses that they used only for racing.

At a rodeo, riders need quick horses for events like calf roping. The horse speeds after a runaway calf while the rider tries to lasso his rope around it.

Rodeos include events for both male and female riders. In the barrel racing event, cowgirls run their horses as fast as they can in a cloverleaf pattern around some barrels. Their horses must be able to turn very quickly.

What would a cowboy be without a horse? Some ranchers and cowboys round up their cattle the same way they always have—on horseback. Many cowboys have American quarter horses because they can easily scramble up hillsides and swim across rivers.

Harness racing is like race walking for horses. They are not allowed to run at full speed, or *gallop*. They must trot toward the finish line as fast as they can. Riders sit in carts called *sulkies* and steer with long reins.

In the game of polo, riders on horseback hit a wooden ball with long-handled mallets. Their polo horses are called *ponies*, no matter how big they are. The best polo ponies follow the ball wherever it goes, without even being told by the rider.

Horses are a big part of the show at the circus. Strong horses pull colorful wagons. Smaller horses circle the ring carrying acrobats on their backs. And beautiful, white horses called *Lipizzaners* can leap and prance just like ballet dancers.

Clip-clop, clip-clop! If you've ever taken a ride in a horse-drawn carriage, you've heard that sound. Before the engine was invented, this was how almost everyone got from place to place. Today, horse-drawn carts and carriages are used mostly for quiet rides through the park or for special occasions.

Horses in parades always look very calm, but it takes a lot of training for them to behave this way. Cheering crowds, whistles, and other loud noises can scare horses. Once a horse has learned to ignore everything but the rider, it is ready to go on parade!

Sometimes big parades include police officers on horseback. Lots of cities have mounted police units. In New York City, they patrol parks and other public areas. Just like parade horses, they are trained to ignore the loud noises of the city.

What would horses be like if they weren't tamed and trained by people? Long ago, all horses were wild animals. They lived and roamed together in big herds.

One kind of wild horse is the *mustang*. Millions of mustangs lived in the American West during the 1800s. But then people began to hunt wild horses, and soon there weren't many left. Today, a law protects all of America's wild horses so they can run free.

There are lots of reasons to love horses! They are gentle, intelligent animals. And people who spend time with lots of horses say they have definite personalities—that each one has a special character and spirit all its own. It is easy to see why horses have always been so important to us, and why they are some of the most popular and well-loved animals of all time.

BABY ELEPHANT

By Lucille Recht Penner
Illustrated by Betina Ogden

On the plains of eastern Africa, a little gray elephant is born. He staggers to his feet. His eyes are red, his head is covered with soft, reddish hair, and his ears are bright pink. He takes a few wobbly steps, trips over his trunk, and sprawls on the ground.

Gently, his huge mother pulls him up with her trunk and front foot.

Other elephants come running. They are the
baby's sisters, aunts, and cousins. The biggest
elephant is the baby's grandmother. She is almost
sixty years old and is the leader of the group.

The elephants sniff the baby, touch him with
their trunks, and rumble softly to welcome him to
the family.

An elephant family is made up of adult females and their children. The young elephants are called calves. There are about twelve elephants in a family. They eat, sleep, and play together. Many families sometimes travel together in a huge herd.

Where is the baby's father? Like most adult male elephants, he lives by himself or with a small group of other males. When the baby is about fourteen years old, he will go off to live on his own, too.

A tall giraffe comes out of the trees. He is curious about the new baby, but the mother elephant won't let him come near. She shakes her head. Her ears make a sharp sound. *Crack!* It's a warning. *Stay away from my baby!*

The baby elephant squeals. He is hungry! His
mother answers with a soft, humming sound.
Then she helps him stand between her front legs
to nurse.

The little elephant reaches only halfway up his
mother's leg, but he already weighs more than
most full-grown men. He curls his trunk over his
head and sucks up his first meal of sweet milk.

The grandmother elephant gives a low, rumbling call, and the other elephants fall into line behind her. She will lead them to the best places to find food and water.

Elephants are very intelligent. They are good at learning and remembering. In some parts of Africa, elephants still walk on paths that were made long ago by their great-great-grandparents.

The new baby walks close beside his mother. He is safe there. She touches him often with her trunk. If he trips and falls, she helps him up and they go on. The whole family walks slowly to make it easy for the baby to keep up.

The baby's older sister walks behind her mother. Sometimes she holds on to her tail with her trunk.

In the forest, the elephants spread out and begin to eat. They call to each other often so that no one gets lost.

Some of the elephants are eating bark. They tear off long strips with their trunks. Others use their tusks to dig up roots.

Tusks are long, pointed, ivory teeth. For many
years, hunters have killed elephants for their
beautiful ivory tusks. Today, Kenya, Zaire, and
other African countries where many elephants
live have laws to protect the elephants from ivory
hunters.

The baby elephant has little baby tusks. When
he is about two years old, they will fall out and his
new tusks will come in. They may grow to be eight
feet long!

An adult elephant eats about 350 pounds of food a day! Elephants need this much food because they are so big. They are the biggest animals in the world, except for whales. The baby's grandmother is almost ten feet tall and weighs one thousand pounds!

Elephants are also very strong. *Smash!* Some elephants ram trees with their heads. They knock them down and eat the tender green leaves on the top branches.

The baby's mother uses her trunk and huge feet to help get food. First she wraps her trunk around a clump of grass and pulls it tight. Then she kicks it. Her strong toenails break right through the grass.

The baby elephant doesn't know how to use his
trunk to pick up food. Instead, he stretches it out
to touch and sniff things. Elephants have an
amazing sense of smell. They can smell water five
miles away!

The baby plays with his trunk, swinging it in
a circle. Sometimes he gets it into his mouth and
sucks it until it falls out again.

An elephant's trunk is really its nose and upper lip. The two small bumps at the tip are used just the way we use our fingers. These elephant "fingers" can pick up a berry or a single blade of grass.

At noon the sun is very hot. The elephant family takes a nap under a clump of tall trees. The adults nap standing up. Some rest their trunks on their tusks. Only their big ears move, flapping back and forth to cool them off.

The baby elephant flops down in the shade
between his mother's legs and falls fast asleep.
She rests her trunk next to his head.

When they wake up, the elephants are thirsty.
They go to the river to drink. A herd of zebras are
already drinking, but they move away to make
room for the elephants.

The baby's mother sucks up a trunkful of water
and squirts it into her mouth. *Aaaaaah!*

Splash! Some of the elephants plunge into the river to swim. Elephants can swim underwater. They hold up the tips of their trunks to breathe.

The mother elephant gives her baby a shower. It feels *good!*

Near the riverbank are pools of thick red mud. Elephants love mud! It feels cool and it's good protection for their skin. An elephant has thick, wrinkly skin, but it is still tender. An insect bite hurts and so does a sunburn. A coat of gooey mud is good protection.

The adults use their trunks to splash mud over themselves, but the calves just jump in and wiggle around. Soon they are the dark red color of the mud.

After their mud bath, the calves play. Some chase each other in circles, squealing and grunting. One runs after a friendly baboon.

Another finds a stick and tosses it in the air.

This little elephant is climbing on his big sister. It is another way elephants play.

As the wind blows through the trees, the grandmother raises her trunk and sniffs the air. The other elephants lift their trunks, too. They smell a lion!

Quickly, the biggest elephants form a tight circle around the calves. They stretch out their great ears, which makes them look enormous. Some of them trumpet and stamp the ground, throwing up clouds of dust. If the lion comes close, they will charge.

But the lion is afraid. He runs away. The elephants are safe.

Now the baby elephant's day is almost over. In the fading light, the family gathers together. One by one, the little calves sink to the ground.

As the stars grow bright, the baby closes his eyes. All around him, the breathing of his family makes a sound like the wind.

BABY CHIMP

By Debra Mostow Zakarin
Illustrated by Betina Ogden

Deep in a forest in central Africa, the sun is just beginning to peek through the trees. As it rises, the animals who live here wake up—colorful birds, tiny tree frogs, leopards, wild pigs . . . and a group of chimpanzees. It is time for them to begin their day.

High in a tree, a mother chimp and her baby are just getting up. The baby chimp climbs out of her nest and swings to the ground. She uses her hands and feet to grab the branches as she goes.

When she gets to the ground, the baby chimp jumps up and down. "Hoo-hoo!" she calls. She wants her mother to hurry up. The rest of their group has already gone to find breakfast.

Chimpanzees live in groups of as many as one hundred. They travel through the jungle and sleep together, but they split into smaller groups to look for food.

Chimpanzees feed mainly on fruit and leaves, but they also like to eat nuts and seeds, tree bark, insects, and eggs. Now and then, they even hunt small mammals such as monkeys, young pigs, and rodents.

The baby chimp and her mother set off to find their breakfast. The baby climbs onto her mother's back. It is her favorite way to travel.

This baby chimp is one year old. She will stay close to her mother until she is about six.

Soon the mother chimp finds a big mound of dirt rising out of the grass. This looks like a good place to get breakfast. She picks up a long, thin twig. This will be her "fishing pole."

What could this mother chimp possibly be fishing for with a twig in a mound of dirt?

The mother chimp is fishing for termites!

The baby looks closely as her mother pokes the twig into the termite tunnel, then slowly pulls it out. It is crawling with termites! The mother chimp picks them off with her lips one by one.

The baby chimp is still too young to fish for termites by herself. But she watches carefully to learn how it is done.

Besides using twigs as "fishing poles," chimpanzees use other "tools" like rocks to crack nuts and open fruit. They are one of the few animals besides humans that are smart enough to make tools.

Chimpanzees belong to the great ape family, along with gorillas and orangutans. But chimps are more like humans than other apes.

gorilla

chimpanzee

orangutan

Like people, chimps are very social animals. The other chimps in their group are very important to them.

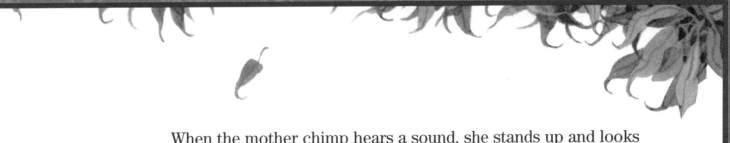

When the mother chimp hears a sound, she stands up and looks around. It is another family. The chimps greet each other with hugs and kisses and excited greeting calls.

The baby chimp likes to play with her friends.

They hang from low branches and jump up and down.

They twirl around and around until they get dizzy.

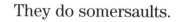

They do somersaults.

Then they all get in a tickle fight and laugh and laugh.

While the babies play, their mothers keep a careful eye on them.
Mother chimps are very protective. They are always ready to step
in if playmates get too rough.

Plip-plop. Suddenly it starts to rain. Play time is over.
The baby chimp climbs into her mother's lap, where it is warm and dry. The mother chimp uses a large leaf to shield her own head from the rain. Then the chimps sit still waiting for the rain to end.

When the rain finally stops, the baby chimp is dry, but her mother is very wet. Still, there is one good thing about the rain . . . .

The mother chimp picks up a leaf. Then, like a sponge, she squeezes fresh, cool water from the leaf into the baby chimp's mouth. The baby licks her lips and opens her mouth wider for another drink.

"*Hoo-hoo-hoo!*" A large male chimp stands up and shakes a tree and screams a warning to the others. There is danger nearby! A hungry leopard.

The baby chimp holds on tight as her mother races with the other chimps up a tall fig tree.

Safely out of the leopard's reach, the chimps wait in the fig tree for the big cat to move on. The leopard is too heavy to climb onto the thin branches where the chimps hide.

Now the baby is no longer frightened. She is much more interested in a midday snack!

Full of tasty figs, the chimps settle down for an afternoon nap.
Some chimps stretch out lazily. But the baby chimp likes snuggling
close to her mother even better.

After her nap, the baby chimp decides it is time to explore. It is always fun to see what the other chimps are doing.

A young chimp is eating some delicious-looking leaves. But he does not want to share. When the baby chimp reaches for some of his dinner, he pushes her away, and the baby starts to cry. Chimps do not shed tears, but they do whimper just like people when they cry.

A chimpanzee's face can show many emotions. An open mouth with no teeth showing means a chimp wants to play or cuddle.

Puckered lips mean a chimp is excited.

Closed eyes and an open mouth mean a chimp is upset.

Lips pulled back and teeth showing might look like a big smile. But this really means a chimp is scared.

The mother chimp hears her baby crying and is there in an instant. She is mad. No chimpanzee can push her baby!

She stands up tall. The young male chimp bows his head and looks away. He knows better than to argue with an angry mother.

The baby chimp and her mother head off to join a group of chimps in a grooming circle. Grooming is a very important part of the chimps' day. It helps them keep their long hair clean, and it is a way to make friends and say, "I like you."

The baby chimp tries to sit still as her mother gently picks dirt and leaves and bugs out of her hair. She likes all the attention. But sometimes grooming tickles!

The baby chimp is tired now. The sun is setting. It is time for bed. One by one, the chimps climb into the trees. The mother chimp picks out a cozy spot for herself and her baby. Then she twists some leaves and branches together to make a new nest for the night.

As the baby chimp closes her eyes, she listens to the chimps around her call out their good nights. "Hoo-hoo-hoo."
Good night, baby chimp.

Baby Whale

By Lynn Wilson
Illustrated by Jean Cassels

In the warm waters near the Hawaiian Islands, a baby whale has just been born.

It is a beautiful day. The rays of the sun shine down through the clear, calm water. Schools of brightly colored fish swim nearby.

But for the newborn whale, the first seconds of life are frightening. He bobs up and down, trying to reach the surface to fill his lungs with air.

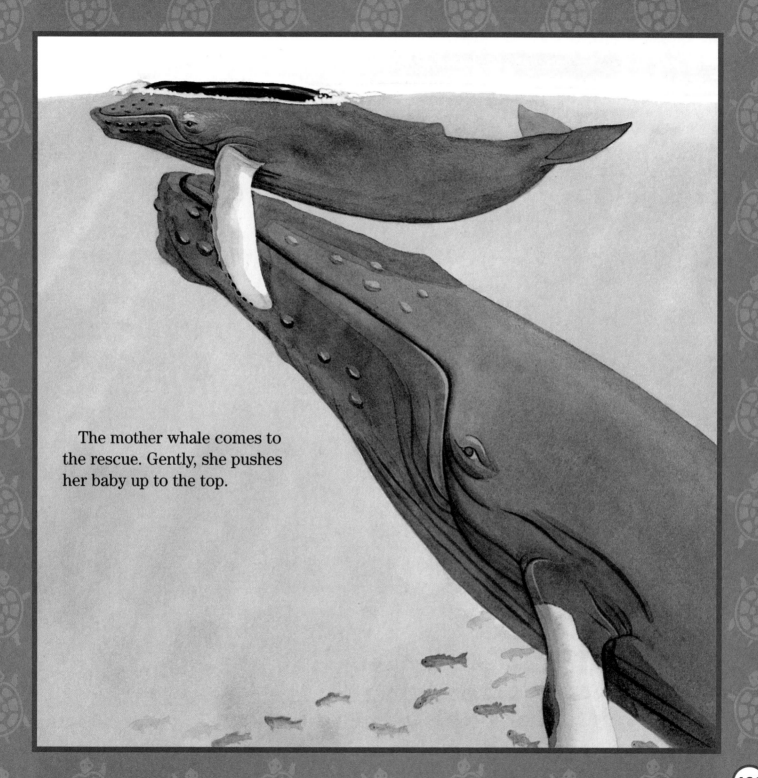

The mother whale comes to the rescue. Gently, she pushes her baby up to the top.

The baby whale takes his first deep breath of air. He breathes in through a hole in the top of his head. This hole is called a *blowhole*.

Now the little whale can stay underwater for a few minutes at a time. When he comes up again, he breathes out through his blowhole.

WHOOSH!

A cone of spray shoots up into the air.

Fish are born knowing how to live in water. But not whales. The baby whale is a mammal, just like a human baby. He cannot breathe underwater. He cannot even swim yet. At first, the mother whale pushes her baby along. If he gets tired, she may even give him a ride on her back.

By the time he is two days old, the baby whale has become a good swimmer. He stays very close to his mother.

The baby and his mother are humpback whales. When a humpback starts to dive, it sometimes waves its long flippers in the air. The flippers look almost like wings. That's why humpbacks are sometimes called "white-winged whales."

The humpback is one of the largest animals in the world. On the day it is born, a baby humpback is already as big and heavy as a car. The mother humpback is more than three times as long.

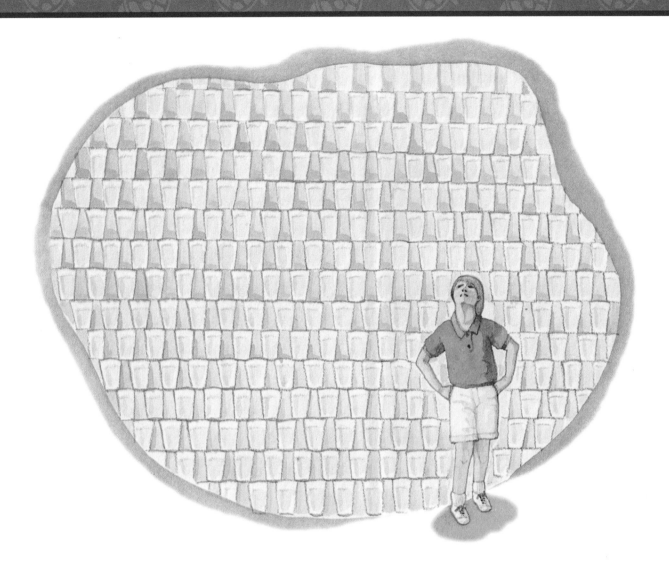

Like other mammals, the mother whale makes milk to feed her baby. When the baby is hungry, she shoots a thick stream of milk into his mouth. A baby humpback drinks a lot of milk. To drink as much, you would have to finish more than 800 glasses of milk every day!

The baby whale spends his days
playing and growing strong.
He practices leaps and backflips.

The little whale is very curious.
He can play for hours with a ball
of seaweed.

Sometimes he even uses
his mother's back as a slide.

To us, the ocean may seem empty. But for a baby whale, the sea is filled with interesting sights and sounds.

Dolphins race along, leaping out of the water as they go. Once in a while, a ship passes nearby. Whales can hear the noise made by the ship's motor from miles away.

There are other strange noises underwater. One day, the baby whale hears a low booming sound. *WHOO-EEE-WHOO-UMP! WHOO-UMP-UMP-UMP!* It is the song of the male humpback whales.

They are looking for females to mate with. All the male humpbacks in this part of the ocean sing the same song. No one knows why.

Sometimes, a male will tag along after a female and her baby. But most of the time, the baby whale and his mother swim alone.

The warm waters near Hawaii are a good place for a baby whale to grow up. But in this part of the ocean, there is not much for a grown-up whale to eat.

By the time the baby whale is six months old, the mother whale is very hungry. It is time for her and the baby whale to swim north, looking for food.

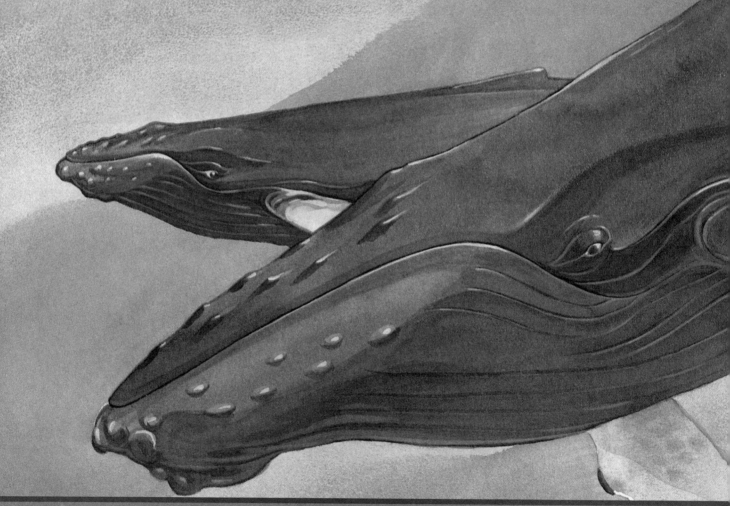

The mother humpback isn't the only hungry animal in the sea.
Groups of killer whales, called *orcas*, roam the ocean looking
for food.

Orcas are hunters. They eat meat.

When a group of orcas spots the baby humpback, they begin
to circle around him.

Suddenly, one orca leaves the group. It heads straight toward the baby whale.

The mother humpback senses the danger. She swims between her baby and the orca.

SPLAT!

She slaps the surface of the water with her big flipper.

The baby whale dives.

His mother swims around, blowing a trail of bubbles. The bubbles make it hard for the orcas to find the baby whale.

Soon the orcas give up and swim away.

Once in a while, a group of orcas will kill and eat a baby humpback. But not this time!

When the orcas are gone, the baby humpback and his mother continue their journey. They are headed for the cold waters off Alaska, almost 3,000 miles away.

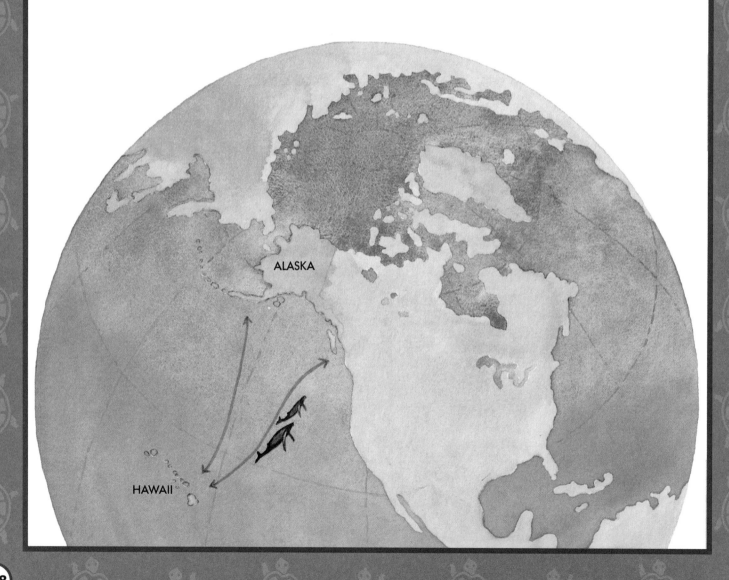

One day, the mother humpback spots a school of fish. She swims underneath it. Once again she starts blowing bubbles.

The fish won't swim through the bubbles. It is almost as if they are caught in a net.

All at once, the mother whale rises up through the ring of bubbles. In one big gulp, she catches hundreds of fish.

Some kinds of whales, like orcas, have teeth. But not humpbacks. A humpback's mouth is filled with long strips, called *baleen*.

Baleen is very much like your fingernails and toenails. It is tough and strong, but it bends a little bit, too. It looks like a thick brush.

When the mother whale takes a big gulp of water, small fish and tiny shrimplike creatures called krill get trapped by her baleen. *WHOOSH!* She spits out the water through the baleen. Then she swallows all the food she has caught.

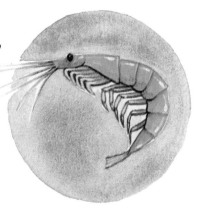

Sometimes a dozen or more humpbacks will feed on the same school of fish. The whales chase after the fish with their huge mouths open wide. There is a lot of splashing and jumping around. Gulls fly overhead, waiting to snap up tiny fish that get tossed into the air.

From far away, it looks as if the whales are fighting, but they are not. The whales are working together to catch as many fish as they can.

The baby whale also is learning to eat krill. He is learning to catch fish with bubble nets. But sometimes he still drinks his mother's milk.

By the time winter comes, the mother whale has grown very fat. Now it's time for her and her baby to make the long journey back to Hawaii.

Once in a while, humpbacks will wait too long to swim south for the winter. The arctic ice closes in around them. If the whales can't get away, they may be attacked by polar bears.

The mother whale and her baby may stay together for a year or more. After that, the baby whale will face many dangers on his own. Most of the dangers are caused by humans.

In some places, fishermen put out big nets under the water. These nets can be over a mile long! A swimming humpback can get tangled up in an underwater net and die.

Oil spills and other kinds of pollution can poison the krill that humpbacks eat.

Even the noisy motors of big ships may scare the humpbacks when they are trying to feed.

If the baby whale is lucky, he will escape all of these dangers. He will live to sing the song of the humpback whale for many years.